DON'T DO THAT!

D0589925

DON'T DO THAT!

by Tony Ross

Mini Treasures

RED FOX

A Red Fox Book

Published by Random House Children's Books
20 Vauxhall Bridge Road, London SW1V 2SA

A division of Random House UK Ltd
London Melbourne Sydney Auckland
Johannesburg and agencies throughout the world

Text and illustrations © Tony Ross 1991

1 3 5 7 9 10 8 6 4 2

First published in the United Kingdom
1991 by Andersen Press

First published in Mini Treasures edition 1999 by Red Fox

The right of Tony Ross to be identified as the author of this work has been
asserted by him in accordance with the Copyright, Designs and Patents Act, 1988.

Printed in Singapore.

RANDOM HOUSE UK Limited Reg. No. 954009

ISBN 0 09 940012 X

Nellie had a pretty nose.

It was so pretty that it won
pretty nose competitions.

It was so pretty that Nellie was given
a part in the Christmas play, with Donna
and Patricia, who had pretty noses too.

"CHILDREN, don't do that!" said teacher.

"It won't come out, sir," said Nellie.
"It's *stuck.*"

The teacher tried to get Nellie's
finger out, but he couldn't.

Neither could the head teacher.
"It's stuck," they said, and sent
Nellie home.

"It's stuck," said Nellie.
"I can get it out," said Henry.
"Mum," shouted Nellie.

But Mum couldn't get Nellie's finger out.
"I can," said Henry.

So Mum called the doctor.
"I can't get it out," he said.
"I can," said Henry.

So the doctor called the police.
"We can't get it out," they said.
"I can," said Henry.

So the police called the conjurer.
"I can't get it out," he said.
"I can," said Henry.

So the conjurer called the farmer.
"I can't get it out," said the farmer.
"I can," said Henry.

So the farmer called the fire brigade.
"We can't get it out," they said.
"I can," said Henry.

Nobody could get Nellie's finger out.
Her nose was longer, and it hurt.
There was only one thing left to do.

"I can get it out," said Henry.

So everybody called the scientist.
"Of course I can get it out," he said...

... "Science can do anything."
And he measured Nellie's nose.
"I can get it out," said Henry.

So the scientist built a rocket ship,
and tied it to Nellie's arm.

Then he tied Nellie's leg to the park bench.

Then he set off the rocket,

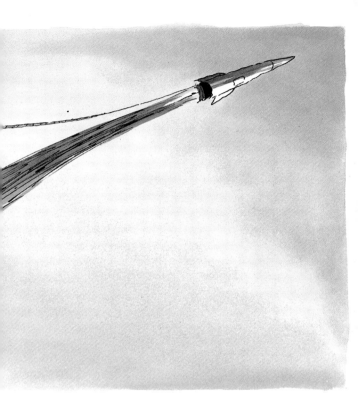

... but Nellie's finger *still* wouldn't come out.

"I can get it out," said Henry.

"Go on then!" said the teachers, Mum, the doctor, the police, the conjurer, the farmer, the fire brigade and the scientist.

So Henry tickled Nellie...
... and it worked!

The
end →